CU00880952

Ann Dale has always had a great interest in science. Upon leaving school, she entered the challenging world of the analytical chemist, where she faced a plethora of demanding analysis each day, to quench her thirst. After previously finding some aspects of science difficult, she understood the need for clarity with the younger generation, especially after working as a teaching assistant in a primary school environment. She now wants to impart her scientific knowledge to a wider audience in a concise yet fun way.

Lots of love

Ann xxx

To Jeanie with grateful thanks, my inspiration.

Ann Dale

SPIKE, SUPER SCIENTIFIC SPIDER INVESTIGATES

AUSTIN MACAULEY PUBLISHERS™

LONDON • CAMBRIDGE • NEW YORK • SHARJAH

A CIP catalogue record for this title is available from the British Library.

ISBN 9781398407459 (Paperback)
ISBN 9781398431980 (ePub e-book)

www.austinmacauley.com

First Published 2022
Austin Macauley Publishers Ltd®
1 Canada Square
Canary Wharf
London
E14 5AA

Note from Author

Subjects covered in this book cover key areas in the ks2 science curriculum

Although specialist vocabulary and technical terminology is applied, all necessary for enriched understanding, subjects are approached in a fun and enquiry manner to aid understanding and help develop a child's own curiosity.

Where applicable, fun facts are given and suggestions for practical activities which supplement the essential tools of observing over the time, pattern seeking, identifying classifying and grouping comparative and fair testing and research using secondary sources.

I aim to spark and inspire that interest in a subject area many children find boring or difficult.

That is how it started for me many moons ago and has become my real passion.

"If you are not willing to learn,
No-one can help you
If you are determined to learn.
No-one can stop you!" Anon.

Living Things

Flora: A Plant
What Fiona Needs to be Healthy
Flower and Reproduction
Classification
Keys
Environment
Life Cycles, Plants
Animals
Humans
Bones and Muscles
Circulation and Heart
Teeth and Eating
Digestion
Healthy Living
Food Chains
Variation
Adaption
Fossils and Evolution

Materials and Their Properties

Rocks

Soil

Solids, Liquids and Gases

Changing State

Water Cycle

Properties of Materials

Electrical Conductivity and Materials

Separating Mixtures

Reversible and Irreversible Changes

Physical Properties

Forces and Magnets

Friction

Air and Water Resistance

Gravity

Levers, Pulleys and Gears

Electricity

Circuit Diagrams

How We See Things

Mirror and Reflections

Shadows

Sound

Earth, Sun and Moon

Hi! I'm spike.

I just love science.

I like learning how things work and why they work.

I love experimenting and investigating, it gets my spider senses singing.

If you find science hard at school or really want to challenge yourself, then follow me through this book.

We can learn and investigate together!

Let's Go!

Living Things

What would you think is a living thing?
Think Along with spike.
What do live things need?
Why do they need them?

Flora: A Plant

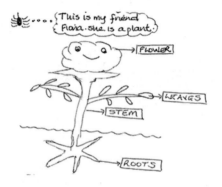

She is a living thing

I have labelled Flora's body parts. Although it is not a body like you and I have.

Flora cannot eat like us.

Do you know how she makes her food?

She makes food in her Leaves

Although she absorbs source some nutrient, for example: minerals up through her roots

Like your body supports you, Flora's stem support her and holds her up to the light. It also carries those minerals and water through Flora's body. Her roots anchor her to the ground. They continue to grow and search for water when it is hot and dry.

Her flower can be colourful and scented or it may be small and hard to notice. Flora has a colourful flower and all the insects, like hoverflies, are attracted to it we will look at why she needs these insects later. I sit nearby-it is a ready meal for me!

Spike says:

Many hundreds of years ago, tulips, a flower which grows in spring time from a bulb: and came from Holland, was worth more than gold!

What Fiona Needs to Be Healthy

When I get hungry, my body is telling me I need food to give me energy. When I'm thirsty, it is water but, what does Fiona need?

Sunlight

Provides light energy to help Fiona make sugars in a process called

Photosynthesis: Using light to help create

Scientists show this in source something called a Formula

$6CO_2+6H_2O$ light energy $\longrightarrow C_6H_{12}O_6+6O_2$ Chlorophyll
Carbon dioxide+water $\longrightarrow$ glucose+oxygen (Sugar)

Chlorophyll is found in Fiona's lovely green leaves.

Nutrients

These are found in the soil where Fiona grows. Minerals are essential to keep her healthy. People help Fiona and other plants by adding minerals to the soil before they plant them, and to help them grow and resist pests and diseases.

Water

This is vital for all life. Like all things, Fiona is made of cells and water is needed to keeps those cells healthy. Minerals are dissolved in water and transported from her roots to all parts of her body.

Water is needed to keep her cells rigid or turgid so she can keep upright on a very hot day, if Fiona is thirsty, she may get limp. This is called wilting.

Air

This is vital for all life. Like you and I, Fiona needs air. She produces oxygen during photosynthesis, but also absorbs it from the atmosphere through special holes in her leaves called stomata, and the oxygen is used for respiration — producing energy for her cells to work.

She uses carbon dioxide, which is absorbed or diffused through these stomata in her leaves, to produce glucose during photosynthesis.

Room to Grow

We all need space. I build my web away from other spiders so I can eat what I want, and whenever an insect comes near. Too many spiders together would compete and that means going hungry and not growing.

Fiona has the same problems. She needs room to grow healthy and receive all the sun, water and nutrients she needs. Too many plants in one place leads to core competition and being unable to walk away, Fiona develop diseases such as mould. This being where her leaves, surrounded by many others, and would not allow air to circulate through.

Think along with spike

Where would you put an indoor plant to grow inside your house?

How would you make this a fair test?

Can you make a prediction on the result?

Can you think of another test you could do to prove plants need nutrients?

How would you carry out this experiment?

(The above is my superstar challenge; see what to do with these at the end of the book.)

An experiment to show how water is transported in plants.

This is known by scientists as translocation, when it is food and nutrients being transported.

When it is a hot and windy day, plants lose excess water, mainly from their leaves, in a process called transpiration.

Apparatus: white flowers, food colouring, beaker, scissors and water.

Method: Fill the beaker with water Add drops of food and nutrients being transported.

Add drops of food colouring, cut flowers stems with scissors and place stems in the water leave for a couple of days.

Can you make a prediction? Fill in the results and conclusion.

Results: The flowers...

I conclude that...

Flowers and Reproduction

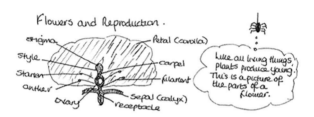

Sepal: outer whorl of leaves protecting the bud

Petals-attract insects

Carpel-stigma, style and ovary produce ovules (unfertilised seeds).

This is how Flora would reproduce:

1. An insect flies along, attracted by her petal's scent and sugary liquid called nectar.
2. The insect feeds on this super energy food, brushing the stamens and catching pollen on its body as it does.
3. It then flies to another flower, which is the same type as Flora, and leaves some of the pollen on this flower's stigma.
4. A pollen tube is formed. The pollen grain travels to the ovary and a new seed is produced with one of the ovules.

5. Many seeds are produced. These will grow into plants similar to Flora.
6. When many seeds are formed Flora loses her petals and the seeds are spread around to grow into healthy young plants.

When an insect visits a plant with another plant's pollen, it is called...

Pollination

When the pollen grain travels down to the ovary and the ovules, it is called...

Fertilization

When the seeds spread around, it is called...

Seed Dispersal

I like to eat insects. Especially big juicy flies, (yum, yum!) but I know you like to be healthy and eat fruit

Spike says:

Did you know that many fruits you eat are a clever way for the plant to disperse seeds?

After the flower dies, the ovary becomes the fruit containing the seeds.

With a strawberry, the seeds are on the outside of the fruit (ovary).

This ensures the seeds are carried away from the parent plant to prevent competition and overcrowding

Not all seeds are eaten though,
Some are dispersed by AIR.

The wind blows the ash seed's wing and helps it fly through the air.

Think Along with Spike

Can you think of another seed that might do this?
Some are dispersed by ANIMALS.

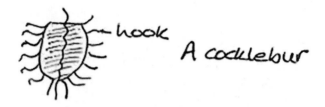

hook

A cocklebur

As the animal walks along, the hooks cling to the animal's fur.

Classification

I'm a living thing. I'm a spider; I have eight legs and a head and body called cepal thorax.

I'm different to you, a bird, an insect, and even Flora. Scientists group all of us that have similar features together.

Birds and mammals breathe using lungs, but one difference is that mammals give birth to live young, whereas birds lay eggs.

This grouping is called classification.

There are seven stages.

Kingdom's Animal and Plants

PHYLUM, from the Greek phylum, meaning 'race'.

Class share common characteristics.

Order grouped with specific characteristics.

Family often descendants of common ancestor in this group. Class share common characteristics

Genus share common characteristics from Latin birth race and stock.

SPECIES, living organisms capable of breeding together living in a similar habitat.

Animals are separated into these individual phyla.

These are examples of each:

ANNELID earthworks

PLATYHELMINTH flatworm

NEMATODE parasitic worm

MOLLUSC snail and slug

Echinoderm starfish

Arthropoda woodlice

ARACHNID spider and scorpion

And the one we are concerned with, Chordata

Think with Spike

There are five kingdoms in the living world. Animals, plants, monera (bacteria), Protista unicellular, single celled animals),

And one other, what could it be?

clue: mushrooms belong to this kingdom.

Chordates are known as vertebrates. They all have a backbone. I am a spider; I have an exoskeleton, which means my skeleton is on the outside.

You have an endoskeleton it is on the inside

I don't have a backbone and I am known as an invertebrate. Classes in the animal kingdom include;

Amphibian cold-blooded, soft skin, live in water and on land...frog

Birds warm-blooded with feathers and wings...sparrow

Fish cold-blooded, scales, fins, gills...cod

Mammals warm-blooded, hair, milk for young...cat

Reptile cold-blooded, dry, scaly skin...snake

Insect 6 legs, paired wings, housefly, my dinner!

I am an arachnid, I have eight legs, unlike flies and insects with a head, thorax and abdomen I have two parts to my body; a head and a cepal thorax.

Spike says:

Did you know another example of an arachnid is a lobster; he has eight legs too.

Superstar Challenge

Can you create an animal which is a vertebrate?

Give it special characteristics and say which class it would belong to in the animal kingdom.

Like animals, plants can be grouped into flowering and non-flowering.

Flowering all produce flowers and would include trees, grasses and Flora and her friends

Non-Flowering include things like ferns, Mosses and Algae.

Keys

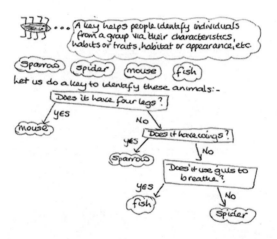

A key helps people identify individuals from a group via their characteristics, habits or traits, habitat or appearance, etc.

Sparrow   Spider   mouse   fish

Let us do a key to identify these animals:-

Does it have four legs?

yes → Mouse

No → Does it have wings?

yes → Sparrow

No → Does it use gills to breathe?

yes → fish

No → Spider

Think Along with Spike

Could you make up a key to identify different animals?

Environment

As a spider, I know how important a clean environment is for me.

I live in a bio diverse ecosystem: a garden.

The gardener maintains my habitat with eco-friendly items.

He does not use chemicals, he is organic and so visiting wildlife, like birds, have lots of worms, insects, and spiders, (eek!), to eat and feed their young.

I have lots of places to live. My niche, where I really fit in, in the garden, is next to Fiona and the garden fence.

The insects she attracts keep me fed.

If the air or the soil becomes polluted then Fiona would not survive; insects would not visit, creatures living in the soil would die out and spiders would have to move away or starve.

A lack of invertebrates would reduce the number and diversity of birds too.

Think with Spike

What effects on the environment do removal of trees and hedgerows have?

Littering on land and sea can kill wildlife.

The animals become trapped in rubbish or eat it and become ill.

Rubbish belongs in bins.

Air pollution not only affects me or other wild life, it can damage buildings; some are weakened and destroyed by acid rain. This also damages and kills trees, causing loss of habitat.

The gardener, where I live, uses natural alternatives; he recycles things and cares for the environment.

Spike Says;

Have you heard of nature reserves?

These are protected areas, where people are not allowed to build and a natural ecosystem is allowed to exist.

Life Cycles, Plants

Like all living things, plants produce young offspring.

Either by wind or animal or visiting insects, pollen from one plant lands on the stigma of another.

The pollen and the egg join in fertilization to make a seed. The seed grows into a seedling.

The seedling grows into a plant. This is sexual reproduction.

Some plants do not need pollen or an egg to reproduce; they reproduce asexually.

An example of this being my friend, Susie strawberry.

She can produce runners which are like tendrils spreading over the ground. These produce new plants called offsets, which can be cut off and planted separately.

Each of these plants will be exactly the same as Susie.

A sexually reproduced plant has characteristics from both parents.

Superstar Challenge

Can you think of pros and cons for sexual and asexual reproduction in plants?

How to take cuttings

We do this to grow a new plant.

1. A small shoot or some small pieces are removed from the parent plant.
2. They are kept in their own micro environment, planted gently in compost around the edge of the

container, moistened with water and placed in a clear plastic bag.

3. The bag must not touch the plants.
4. They are placed in a cool place not cold.
5. Water should be seen as a mist on the inside of the bag after a few days.
6. After a few weeks, remove the bag if the plants have new leaves and have grown then carefully remove them and pot them up into their own pot and fresh compost.

Take care with those young new roots.

Animals

Mammals give birth to live young.

Chickens, fish insects, all birds, in fact and spiders lay eggs. My gardener friend likes to keep chickens in the garden. Unfortunately, they fancy spiders as a snack I keep out of their way.

A father animal produces sperm when he mates with the mother animal. His sperm fertilise her eggs, ova and this then develops into their offspring.

A human baby takes nine months to develop inside its mother. This is called gestation.

When a baby grows inside its mother, she is pregnant. Birth is when a baby is born.

Spike Says:

Baby spiders are called spiderlings my mother carried us on her back when my brothers, sisters and I were born.

The life cycle of a mammal:

Think Along with spike:

Can you draw out the life cycles of a pig, a cat and a dog?

The life cycle of a bird:

Ducks have ducklings, geese have goslings, swans have cygnets.

The life cycle of an insect:

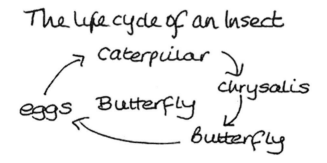

Humans

A human like you goes through a series of stages in their lifecycle.

When you are born, you are a baby

As you learn to walk and talk, you become a toddler. You start school as a child and stay as a child until a process called puberty, when you become an adolescent.

In your late teens, you start adult life. When you retire from work, you enter old age. During puberty, chemicals called hormones race round your body.

Girls find their hips widening, breasts developing, periods starting as ova are produced and pubic grows.

Boys find their voice gets deeper, facial and pubic hair grows, shoulders and chest broadens, whole body becomes more muscular, the penis enlarges and the testes begin to produce sperm.

Bones and Muscles

I have an exoskeleton. It is on the outside of my body.

Your skeleton is inside your body-endoskeleton. To help your bones grow, you need calcium, which can be found in dairy products and vitamin D. Plenty of sunshine will help with that!

Bones help support and protect your body organs and work with your muscles to help keep you active.

Your bones include:

Cranium: skull protect brain and facial organs
Cervical: vertebrate neck support the neck and head
Scapula: shoulder blade
Clavicle: collarbone
Sternum: breastbone
Rib (12 pairs): protect chest area
Humerus: upper arm bone

Radius: lower arm bone

Ulna: lower arm bone

Carpals: wrist bone

Metacarpals: hand bones

Phalanges: finger and toes

12 thoracic: vertebrate chest support the back

5 Lumbar: vertebrate lower back

5 fused sacral: vertebrate base of spine

Coccyx: tail bone

Pelvis: protection

Femur: thighbone

Patella: kneecap

Tibia: shinbone

Fibula: lower leg

Metatarsals: foot bones

Tarsals: ankle bones

Some bones are also used to make red blood cells.

Spike Says:

Did you know, there are 33 vertebrae in your back bone which protect the spinal cord, support the head and have the pelvis and rib cage attached.

Bones, move as joints.

Hinge joint e.g. the knee,

Gliding joint e.g. the wrist,

Ball and socket joint e.g. the hip,

Bones are cushioned by cartilage.

Spike Says:

Did you know, your ears and the end of your nose are made of cartilage?

Muscles

Skeletal or voluntary muscles.

These can flex or extend When you want to move your arm or leg. Then nerves stimulate these muscles to help perform these actions.

Smooth or Involuntary Muscles

You have no control of these muscles as they perform important jobs in the body, for example, in the blood vessels and intestines.

Cardiac Muscle

Able to produce electrical impulses to keep the heart beating. Muscles other relaxes.

They are called ANTAGONISTIC.

The Biceps and TRICEPS in the arm.

When you bend your arm, the biceps contracts and the triceps relax.

When you straighten your arm, the triceps contract and the biceps relax.

What is a TENDON?

A tendon acts like an elastic band and joins bones to muscles. This allows the contracting muscle to lift or lower or extend parts of the body via the bones.

Think Along with Spike

Lift your hand and move it towards your face; what do you feel?

Can you feel your muscles working?

Circulation

This is the transport system of your body.

This is the transport system of your body.

It consists of the heart, blood and blood vessels. The systemic system carries oxygen around the body to the heart.

The pulmonary system carries carbon dioxide to the lungs and collects oxygen, ready to pump it round the body.

Blood Vessels

These are made of elastic and smooth involuntary muscles. They are like hollow tubes and the inside is the Lumen.

Artery

These are thick walled vessels which mainly carry blood away from the heart

Veins

These are thick walled vessels which also contain valves to help keep the blood moving along. They mainly carry blood to the heart.

Capillaries

These are thin walled vessels which connect veins and arteries. Some are so narrow that they only allow one red blood cell through at a time. Being thin, they allow movement or diffusion of gases between blood cells and tissues of the body.

Blood

Spike Says:

Blood is put into groups: A, B, AB, and O. Rhesus Ca protein found or not found in blood) positive or negative.

Do you know your blood type?

Blood, yours is red due to the mineral (iron).

It consists of:

Red Blood Cells

Have no nuclei, unlike other cells.

Are called biconcave by scientists, which gives them a high surface area to collect and carry move oxygen, and live just 120 days.

Those which contain oxygen are oxygenated and make blood appear bright in colour.

Those lacking oxygen but containing more waste carbon dioxide are deoxygenated.

They are replaced by bone marrow.

White Blood Cells

These are also made in the bone marrow and help the body's immune system. They often immobilise germs, or even eat them by enclosing and destroying them. Whenever you cut yourself, white blood cells travel directly to the wound

Plasma

This helps keep blood fluid and is mainly produced from food and water.

Nutrients

Carried in the transport system to where they are needed, for example, stored glucose needed as energy by an exercising muscle.

Hormones

Special chemical messengers in the blood needed to help certain parts of the body to work.

Platelets

Also made in the bone marrow and help your blood clot when you cut yourself.

Other Waste Materials

For example, urea.

Spike Says:

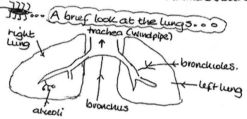

The bronchioles are like branches on a tree, having divided from the trunk the bronchus.

The trachea carries oxygen and carbon dioxide to and from the lungs.

At the end of the bronchioles are air sacs, called alveoli.

These are moist, thin walled and have high surface area.

Oxygen from lungs passes into blood.

Carbon dioxide to lungs and breathed out.

Alveoli are covered in tiny capillaries that join up to the rest of the circulatory system.

All veins and arteries are important in the body, but we will look at those concerned with the heart and circulation.

(Superior) Vena Cava

Largest vein in the body. All deoxygenated blood flows through this to the heart. It flows upward against gravity. The superior vena cava runs from upper body to heart.

(Inferior) Vena Cava

From lower body to heart.

PULMONARY ARTERY.

Takes blood to the lungs.

Aorta

The main artery carrying blood from the heart around the body; oxygenated blood. It is very thick-walled as it is put through a lot of force. It flows down with gravity, first running to the upper body, then loops down behind the heart to the lower body.

Heart

It is found between the lungs, in the middle of the chest.

It is inside a special sac called pericardium.

It is a pump in one!

The right side receives blood from the body and pumps it to the lungs.

The left side receives blood from the lungs and pumps it out to the lungs.

It is capable of producing its own electrical signals, to keep the cardiac muscle pumping blood, by squeezing it, (heartbeat).

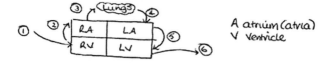

A atrium (atria)
V ventricle

45

Spike Says:

At rest, it takes six seconds... The heart is split into four chambers—two arteries and two ventricles.

They are separated by valves, which act like doors between the atria and ventricle.

These valves open to let blood move ahead and close quickly to stop it flowing backwards.

They create the hub-dub sound we hear.

The hub being the mistral and bicuspid valves.

The dub being the aortic and pulmonary valves.

The valves themselves are controlled by the heartstring.

The left side of the heart is responsible for blood pressure.

It is the largest and most muscular part as it pumps blood out to the body.

Experience with your pulse.

Using your index finger, find your pulse on your wrist or your neck.

Count the beats you feel as you rest, for one minute.

Jump on the spot or skip for one minute, then take your pulse again.

How do you explain the difference?

Spike Says:

Amazing blood facts!

- One drop of blood contains approximately five million red blood cells.
- Blood travels 40 cm per second through the aorta.

- Your heart pumps round 23,000 drops litres of blood a day.
- All your blood vessels in your body would measure around the earth 2.5 times.

Phew! Need a rest after that.

Teeth and Eating

Teeth, the first stage of digestion, cutting and grinding food.

When you are young, you have twenty milk teeth.

After a while, these teeth fall out and are replaced by your permanent teeth. These last teeth must be cleaned and cared for, as they cannot be replaced.

The parts of a tooth:

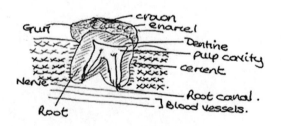

Tooth Decay

Sugary foods and acidic food and juice can attack the enamel. If this happens plaque can form, and if teeth are not brushed correctly with toothpaste, then this can lead to tooth decay and tooth loss.

Regular dental visits to have your teeth checked ensure they are healthy.

Types of Teeth

Molar: larger surface area to similar premolar for crushing and grinding.

Canine

For tearing

Incisor

Bite and cutting

Spike Says:

Did you know that there are 32 teeth in a permanent dentition? Why are the last four molars to appear called wisdom teeth?

What is a carnivore, omnivore and herbivore?

Digestion

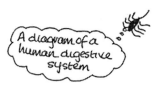

A diagram of a human digestive system

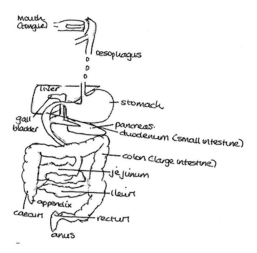

Food is ground up and chewed by teeth in the mouth.

It is flicked to the back of the throat and swallowed.

It travels down the oesophagus to the stomach.

Food is constantly being digested in the stomach and from here, it is gradually released, (sometimes after it has been in the stomach for four hours), by a valve; the phyloric sphincter to the small intestine. Digested food-nutrients are absorbed here into tiny blood capillaries, (fat is absorbed by a special organ called lacteal)

The remaining digested mixture passes to the large intestine.

This contains bacteria that break down any remaining food, makes important vitamins and absorbs a lot of water.

Waste (faeces) travels through the rectum to the anus.

Food moves through the digestive system in a series of waves called peristalsis where muscles contract and relax.

Special chemicals called enzymes speed up digestion.

They are found all through the digestive system and are specific to what they do.

They depend on acid and alkali conditions and temperature.

Body temperature being the optimum for them to work.

Spike says; ugh alert!

Do you know how a spider eats a fly?

Often, we poison the fly and wrap it up in silk.

Then, most of us inject digestive juices into it with our fangs and turn into a type of fly soup…yummy!

Healthy Living

I eat and live very healthy, lots of fresh food and fresh air.

You need to have lots of exercise, some fresh air every day and eat a balanced diet.

Too many sugary foods will not give you the nutrients that you need.

A balanced diet should include:

CARBOHYDRATES	potatoes, rice, provide energy
PROTEIN	Fish, meat, tofu growth and body repair.
FATS	Cheese, olive oil, long term energy.

Some fats are better than others and should only be a small part of your diet.

MINERALS: Dairy, meat, fruit veg various uses.

Trace minerals are needed in small amounts, but are very important.

Potassium and sodium chloride, (KCl, NaCl), are trace minerals containing trace elements, potassium (K) and sodium (Na), iron (Fe), is vital for blood. A lack of it causes a disease called anaemia.

VITAMINS: meat, vegetables, fruit, various uses.

Vitamin	Found in	Use
A	Carrots	Night vision, eyesight.
B complex	yeast, cereal, liver	Body maintenance.
C	Veg, fruit (esp citrus)	Healthy Body
D	Act of sunshine on skin, also oily fish, dairy	Healthy bones and teeth
E	wholemeal bread, dairy	Healthy body
K	cereal, liver, fruit, nuts	Blood clotting

WATER: essential to keep the body healthy and hydrated.

FIBRE: cereal vegetables, healthy digestive system.

Fibre includes both soluble and insoluble.

As I said earlier, exercise is important to keep you and your heart healthy. It also keeps your mind healthy.

Unhealthy living includes watching too much television or working on a computer for too long in one session; eating too many un – healthy foods-some are OK as a treat – and adults who drink lots of alcohol and smoke cigarettes.

These actions are damaging the body.

Food Chains

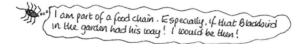

I am part of a food chain. Especially, if that Blackbird in the garden had his way! I would be then!

In a healthy environment and bio diverse ecosystem, food chains can easily be found.

Many food chains combined can create a food web.

For example;

Grass ⟶ Rabbit ⟶ Fox

Rabbits eat grass and a fox would eat a rabbit.

Flower ⟶ Hoverfly ⟶ Spider ⟶ Blackbird ⟶ Cat

If there were huge numbers of flowers in the garden, then there would be lots of hover flies, attracted by the flowers and their nectar, for me and other spiders to eat.

This would increase the number of blackbirds, and maybe bring in extra cats.

Each species is dependent on the other.

This interdependence determines the number of each species found. We need each other!

At the start of every food chain is a PLANT, like my friend, Fiona.

The sun provides the light and energy plants need to create their food.

It is the producer in the food chain.

In my food chain there are four consumers.

The hoverfly is a primary consumer.

The spider is a secondary consumer.

The blackbird is a tertiary consumer.

The cat is a quaternary consumer (sounds very technical!)

This just means that all consumers rely on the producer to start the food chain and then consume each other.

The blackbird is the prey of the cat.

The spider is the prey of the blackbird.

The hoverfly is the prey of the spider.

But the spider is the predator of the hoverfly.

The blackbird is the predator of the spider.

The cat is the predator of the blackbird…phew!

There are more producers than consumers.

The higher up the chain the consumer is, the smaller in number they become.

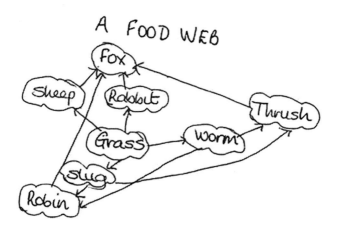

This shows how species are inter-dependent on each other.

Superstar Challenge

Can you create your own food webs?

What would happen if one of the consumers was not there anymore?

What would happen if the producer died out?

Variation

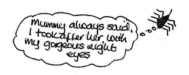

You are the offspring of your mom mum and dad.

You have inherited features from them.

Differences between you and your mom mum or dad are called variations.

You are made up of cells, far too many for this spider to count. Your cells carry information called genes.

Genes come from your mum and dad. These genes decide if you have blue or brown eyes, blonde or brown hair, for example. These are what you have inherited.

Some genes are more dominant than others and so, you may have dark hair if your mom has blonde hair.

You may look like Granny or Granddad with a pointy chin, or long nose. This is because this information was passed onto your parents and then passed onto you.

Adaption

Animals and plants live in habitats. Habitats can be hot or cold, dry, wet, icy, vary in temperature, etc.

Animals evolve to be able to catch and eat food and survive in the most efficient way.

A famous Scientist called Charles Darwin is noted for his work on evolution.

This is where, over many years, slight changes to the animal have helped it survive.

Those unable to evolve would often become extinct.

Environmental changes lead to changes in genes, over many generations, helping the animal adapt.

Adaption being very important if there is competition for food or they are likely to become food themselves and die out.

Spike Says:

During the Victorian era, industrialisation became greater. Coal burning created smoke and soot. This landed on trees, turning their bark black. The white peppered moth stood out against the black bark and was prey of many birds. Gradually, they evolved and became black.

This helped them to camouflage themselves. They adapted and survived

Cleaner air meant a reduction of soot, cleaner trees and the moth adapting again as a white moth.

Some animals are very specialised and are only adapted to live in one particular habitat for example others.

Other animal is more general and can live in different habitat for example red fox.

Weasel family members show adaptation to different habitats. Though closely related, they look very different.

Others live near water.

Badgers live in woodland underground homes.

Pine marten live up in woodland tress.

Superstar Challenge

Can you create an animal and describe how it is adapted to the habitat it lives in?

Animals show physical adaptions, for example types of teeth behavioural too.

Are they nocturnal (hunting at night)? Do they hibernate?

Are they social (Hunting in packs)? Or solitary (Where prey may be scarce)?

Think with Spike

What features does a Barn owl have to help it hunt its prey, (like mice) at night?

Fossils and Evolution

These are great evidence of how animals have evolved to adapt to their environment

When an animal or plant died, its remains would become buried under layers of mud, soot and sand. This, in turn, over a long time, would harden as rock.

Most fossils are found in sedimentary rock. This is because they and their characteristics are preserved.

Sedimentary rode being a 'soft' rode of Limestone sandstone, clay or shale or strata (layers) of all these

Trace fossils include footprints.

Fossilised tree sap is called amber. Coal is made of fossilised plants. Chalk is made of fossilised skeleton of marine animals.

Spike says

A famous palaeontologist, (Fossil's Scientist) made important findings of fossils. Her name was Mary Anning She found an Ichthyosaurus in Lyme Regis, where she lived.

A real pioneer!

Materials and Their Properties

What could materials mean?

Why did I find all of these?

Rocks

Our planet is covered in rocks.

Rocks are made of minerals.

There are three main types of rock and they all take part in the rock cycle but not always following this order.

Rock Cycle:

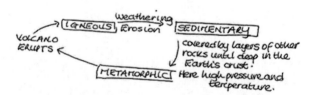

In the Earth's crust, high temperature and pressure build up, and along with movement of special plates, called tectonic plates, causes a volcano to erupt.

Toxic gases and hot molten rock, called lava, is thrown into the air or just pours along the ground.

This cools into Magma.

After a certain time Igneous ('of e'fire) rock is formed for example, basalt (above ground) and granite (below the surface).

Rain, sun and wind break up this rock into smaller parts (erode by weathering).

These parts form sediment and layer like a sandwich in the bottom of a river. They become compact and hard as the layers continue to build up. SEDIMENTARY

For example; shale limestone and sandstone.

Gradually over many years, this rock makes its way down in the Earth's crust and become metamorphic rock.

Metamorphic Rock

The high temperature and pressure hardens other rocks, for example Limestone becomes marble, and shale becomes slate or granite.

Properties

Marble (metamorphic) is very hard; it won't absorb water and is called impermeable.

Sand stone (Sedimentary) is very soft; it readily absorbs water and is called permeable.

Soil

Wind carries small pieces away, some as small as dust. These fragments, along with organic matter, help to create soil. These fragments also contain important minerals that some animals and plants need to keep healthy.

There are many 'types' of soil, depending on the types of particles creating them.

These include CLAY, SALT and SAND.

Clay is made from small particles that are linked closely together, are tightly-packed and when wet, have a very sticky texture.

Silt-loam is the perfect soil for my gardener. It is made of roughly equal amounts of clay and sand.

Sand is made of larger particles. These tend to have some air-spaces between them and are not as tightly packed as clay.

Soil is made of clay, silt organic matter, water, sand, air, animals and minerals

Think with Spike

What do think 'organic matter' means?

Animals in soil not only include invertebrates like beetles and earthworms, but also fungi and microbes or bacteria.

Soil is called a dynamic natural resource because it constantly erodes (or wears a way) and re-creates.

Spike Says:

Did you know that the moment rock is exposed to the environment, it starts to become soil?

Not only does weathering affect rocks,

Weathering creates a physical change, smaller fragments plants called Lichens, also wear the rock surface down.

Chemical change is where the rock dissolves in rain or reacts in air

Biological change: birds, animals and plants take up minerals and add organic fungi and for example, woodlice turn the organic into nutrients.

Soil is vital not just for providing plants with nutrients and anchorage, but release trapped carbon dioxide gas into the atmosphere. It is involved in nutrient cycles and helps to filter and clean water.

Soil is layered into horizons. This could look like this:

Organic/humus leaves twigs,

Topsoil organic and minerals plants and animals' subsoil,

Subsoil day, iron and organic matter,

PARENT MATERIAL: Large rock,

BED Rock Large mass of rock.

An Experiment to identify your soil type:

Fill an empty plastic bottle half-full with water.

Add a spoonful of soil.

Replace lid on the bottle and shake.

Let the mixture settle for 5–10 minutes.

Check for the components that make up the soil, being shown in layers in the bottle.

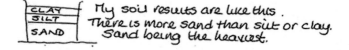

My soil results are like this. There is more sand than silt or clay. Sand being the heaviest.

Superstar Challenge

Could you think of an experiment to see which soil type would allow water to pass through most easily? How would you ensure it is a fair test?

What is the only variable being tested here?

Could you predict which it would be before carrying out the test and why?

Solids, Liquids and Gases

These are also known as states of matter. There are another two known states of matter, one of which I shall tell you a little bit about, later.

Think with Spike you identify which are solids, liquids and gases from this following list?

Oxygen, water, sponge, wood, rice, iron, tar, ice, cooking oil, syrup, carbon dioxide, lemonade.

Everything, and I mean everything, is made of atoms. These are very small.

Spike Says:

Scientists believe there are more atoms in a grain of sand than stars seen in the universe.

There are approximately five hundred quadrillion atoms in a speck of dust, (atchoo!) wow!

In a solid, these atoms are very close together, and stay linked together, like animals huddled together in the cold.

In a liquid, these atoms are still together, but move more freely; they are linked together like children holding hands but not needing to be huddled together, as they are feeling warmer.

In a gas, the atoms distance themselves from each other. They spread around the area they are in and constantly move and run into each other.

You can pour a liquid into different containers. This liquid will change shape when you move it around in a container and adapt to the shape of the container it went in, but its volume remains the same.

Solids do not change shape when they are moved, they are unable to adapt and have the scarce volume.

Gases have the same shape and volume of any container they are in.

Different materials make solids. These include glass, plastic, wood, wool etc.

Liquids can be poured and include water, oil, treacle, and washing up liquid etc. Oil, treacle, washing up liquid etc.

Not all liquids behave the same when they are poured along a flat surface held at an angle.

Thicker liquids are stickier and are called more viscous than thinner liquids.

An Experiment to Identify Viscosity

Using a chopping board or a similar flat surface, gently pipette the same amount of various liquids separately on the board, keeping the board flat.

Liquids can include water, washing up liquid, golden syrup, lemonade, cooking oil, etc.

When all have been placed on the board, gently cut it and time how long it takes for them to travel to the other side.

Which is the fastest and why?

Viscous liquids are also very dense. They are heavier than water. This is called density.

Gases are mainly invisible and for example, air is always surrounding us.

Air is a mixture of different gases, including oxygen, carbon dioxide, nitrogen, some inert gases, exhaust gases (if near vehicles) and water in its gaseous state.

Changing State

I said just now that solids, liquids and gases and the others, (I haven't forgotten, I will mention it at the end of this chapter) are states of matter.

When they change, a physical change has occurred and a solid, like chocolate, when heated, will change to a liquid.

A liquid for example, petrol is dangerous, because when it is warmed and the outside temperature is warmed, it will change to a gas.

Some changes like a raw egg being fried to a cooked egg, (liquid solid), is an irreversible change.

When chocolate is heated, and then cooked again (solid→ liquid solid), it is a reversible change.

An experiment to identify which temperature various types of chocolate melt at:

Plain chocolate, milk chocolate, white chocolate and cooking chocolate.

Equal amounts of each of the above are put in separate beakers.

A thermometer measures the temperature of the water as it heats up and as each chocolate melts, at exactly the same point, that temperature is recorded.

This is the melting point of the chocolate and when it has changed from the solid to the liquid phase.

Draw an annotated diagram of the equipment used.

Can you write results out in a table?

Chocolate will melt at different temperatures as different types contain different quantities of ingredients.

White chocolate contains more sugar and milk than plain chocolate.

When a solid is heated, it melts and becomes a liquid.

Taking ice as the solid at room temperature; ice will melt into a liquid: water.

When a liquid is heated, bubbles of gas are formed and water vapour or steam is produced. Water boils at 100° C.

This water vapour is released into the surrounding air, but as soon as it hits something cold, like a mirror, water droplets form as the gas molecules and atoms gather together.

When atoms of gas cool and gather together they condense into a liquid.

Water vapour gas has condensed to water, the liquid state when a liquid is cooled and cooled, it frees into a solid.

Water freezes at 0° C. The long chain of atoms huddles together and forms a solid: ice.

Some gases won't form a liquid.

Instead, they go directly from gas ⟶ solid state

At -79° C (brrrr!), carbon dioxide gas freezes and forms its solid state, commonly called dry ice.

They will also change from a solid ⟶ gas state.

As soon as dry ice is exposed to the air, it will change to a gas.

This process is called SUBLIMATION.

Superstar Challenge

Can you explain how you know that sand is a solid even though you can pour it like a liquid?

Spike Cays:

Corn flour and water, and honey itself, are example of Non-Newtonian fluids. Under pressure, they behave as solids, but without that, they will pour off a spoon like a liquid.

Spike Says:

A little about plasma.

Plasma is the most common state of matter. It is basically charged gas, and is where parts of an atom, called electrons, are removed, carrying a negative charge. They exist at the same time as the remainder of the atom, a positive charge.

This ionises the gas, creating a great deal of energy and, in turn, creating more ionizing.

The sun is a massive plasma star; an ionised ball of hydrogen and helium gases, which are as atoms, constantly gaining and losing electrons. This creates a great deal of heat, or thermal energy, the light and heat we need to survive.

Water Cycle

Before we investigate this, let us think about that dreadful washing line in the garden. Spiders keep away; they are not the perfect place to await lunch. I learnt that the hard way.

Why do you put wet clothes out on a washing line?

To dry! I hear you shout OK. But what does dry mean, what happens? When does that washing dry best?

Drying is when all the water has evaporated from the clothes, changing from liquid in your clothes, to water vapour, a gas in the air.

Washing will dry best on a sunny day, when the temperature is high: as it is faster to change water from a liquid to a gas state.

Also, if it is windy, the wind will blow the water vapour away from the drying clothes; if the vapour remains in the air surrounding the clothes then evaporation is slower, as the air is humid and saturated with water vapour.

Pegging the clothes out increases their surface area which also speeds up evaporation.

Now the water cycle.

All the water on this planet has been here for many, many years, even the dinosaurs were alive.

It is just recycled. it is not freshly created constantly.

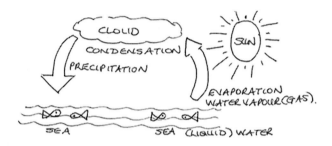

Water in the sea is heated by the sun.

It changes from a liquid gas, → evaporation.

The water vapour rises through the air.

Higher in the atmosphere, this gas cools.

It changes from a gas → liquid, condensation.

The water droplets formed from the water vapour come together, creating clouds. As more and more group together, they become heavier and heavier.

The water from the clouds falls back into the sea as RAIN, HAIL, or SNOW precipitation.

Properties of Materials

I create a very tough, flexible and light material spider silk.

Plastic, wood, metal, paper, fabric are just a few examples of material.

Materials are used everywhere. Their unique or special properties make them perfect for jobs that they are used for.

Even a spider, like me, knows that a house made out of fabric would not be useful, as the fabric would not be as hard, tough or durable as wood or brick. It would also be susceptible to weathering.

Think with Spike

I have given you some materials and a property of them.

Can you think of a use for them and why you would use them for that?

Fabric opaque
Cork thermal insulator
Marble hard
Glass transparent
Cotton wool soft

Can you think of any other properties these materials may also have?

Certain materials are used because they are good conductors of heat.

These include metals, for example: copper, steel and aluminium.

Saucepans, used for cooking and heating food, are often made of these.

However, because they are good at conducting heat, they are not good at retaining or keeping it. A hot drink in a metal cup would soon go cold.

Insulators of heat include wood, plastic or polystyrene.

They are poor conductors, and will not lose heat to the surroundings. They would be safer to be used as a saucepan handle than metal, as heat would not be conducted along them, but practically, they would easily burn, so are not used.

However, plastic or polystyrene cups are often used for hot drinks, as they insulate and retain the heat, so the drinks stay hot.

An experiment to see which type of materials keeps a drink hot:

Using a plastic, polystyrene, metal, paper and ceramic cup of the same size and volume, pour in an equal volume of hot liquid, get an adult to help with this.

With a thermometer, measure the initial (starting) temperature.

After five minutes, take the temperature of each liquid in each cup and record the results.

Also, take note of the air temperature (WHY?).

Plot the results on a bar chart.

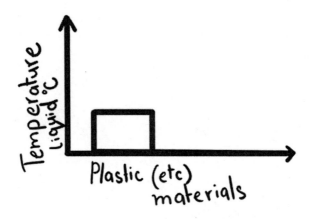

Are your results what you expected them to be? Why?

What effect does air temperature have, on a hot day or a cold day, on your cups of liquid?

Electrical Conductivity
and Materials

Some materials conduct electricity. Some are insulators and don't conduct.

We will look at electricity in detail later.

Electricity is caused by the movement of electrons.

An electric charge is the movement of a charge in metals: a negative charge, as the electrons move.

Conductors of electricity would include metals, for example: aluminium, steel and brass.

These contain a large number of electrons: which are free to move and carry an electric current.

Insulators would include, for example, china, plastic and glass.

These have few, if any charges, (very few free electrons able to move).

Some insulators can be electrically charged, as in static electricity. When these materials are rubbed, electrons form surface atoms on an object, but do not charge the whole object, only the surface.

Some materials are also attracted by a MAGNET.

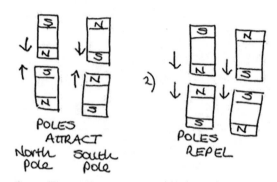

POLES ATTRACT
North Pole   South Pole

POLES REPEL

All magnets have a magnetic field around them, and a magnetic force between them, as these forces interact.

Any metal which can be magnetised for example, iron, nickel and cobalt, would magnetise when placed in a magnetic field. They can form permanent or temporary magnets themselves.

The movement of electrons would also create a magnetic field in a process called electromagnetism.

The first law of magnetism states that unlike poles, (where the magnetic force is concentrated), attract each other. Like poles repel.

This is indicated in my magnet diagram.

Think Like Spike

Could you write an experiment showing how you would separate a mixture of metals and non-metals with a magnet?

Would all metals be magnetised? Why?

Spike Says:

Did you know that many migrating birds may use the earth's magnetic field to guide them?

Separating Mixtures

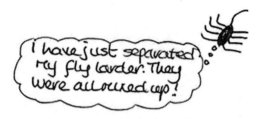

I have just separated my fly larder. They were all oured up!

A mixture contains more than one solid, liquid or gas.

Air is a mixture of gases.

A cup of white tea, (sweetened), is a mixture of tea leaves, hot water, milk and sugar.

A mixture of solid could include gravel, sand and rock jumbled together.

Some mixtures are things put together, but are still easily removed in order to separate them.

With our solid mixture, a sieve could remove the sand from the mixture, as only the grains of sand would go through the sieve.

A mixture of pasta, cooked in hot water, would separate the cooked solid from the liquid using a colander.

Freezing air at different temperatures would separate the gases.

Some solids form mixtures with water by dissolving in it.

These include salt, sugar, coffee, bath salts and bicarbonate of soda.

If the water is heated and the solid added whilst stirring, then the solid dissolves quickly.

If lots of solid, for example, salt, is added to a beaker of water, and stirred until no more solid will dissolve and lots of solid is left in the water, then this is called a saturated solution. Here, the water cannot dissolve any more of the salt. The undissolved salt remains at the bottom of the beaker.

When a solid dissolves in a liquid, it forms a solution.

The salt is called the solute and the water the solvent.

This can be represented in a chemical formula:

$NaCl(S) + H2O (L) \longrightarrow Na+(aq) + Cl-(aq)$
(s) is solid (l) is liquid.
Na+(aq) are sodium ions in water.
Cl-(aq) are chloride ions in water.

Salt water can be separated into salt and water by the following method:

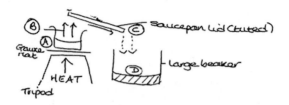

A. The beaker containing a solution of dissolved salt in water is placed on top of a gauze mat, which is itself placed over a tripod and Bunsen burner.

B. A saucepan lid is placed above this and tilted, with one end directly above a large beaker.

C. The burner is lit and the solution heated and gently summered. Once at 100° C

D. Steam, as water vapour, is seen rising into the air, as it evaporates from the solution.

E. This steam hits the cold saucepan lid and condenses into water liquid. The water forms droplets.

F. Which then fall into the large beaker.

G. The water collected in the large beaker would be very pure.

The beaker being heated would have a solid remaining behind; this being salt (and any impurities that may have been in the water before).

If you have sand in water, then the sand sits at the bottom of the container. The sand will not dissolve in water and is insoluble.

To separate these, we could filter them.

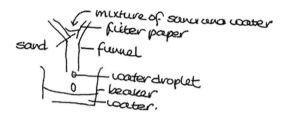

A filter funnel is lined with a filter paper. The mixture is poured in; the sand is collected as the solid in the filter paper. The liquid water would pass through into the beaker underneath.

Spike Says:

Scientists react chemicals together and produce solids and liquids as the result.

The solid produced is called the precipitate and the liquid is the filtrate.

Silver nitrate solution + sodium chloride solution $\longrightarrow$ silver chloride solid (precipitate) + sodium nitrate (filtrate)

$AgNO_3$ (aq) + NaCl(aq) $\longrightarrow$ AgCl(s) + $NaNO_3$(aq)

Some liquids are called miscible as they mix together by diffusion, where one liquid spreads itself from its higher concentration through the lower concentration of the other liquid.

For example, blackcurrant squash and water.

Atoms of blackcurrant squash would diffuse into the water, where there are no atoms of blackcurrant squash immiscible liquids stay separate.

When small particles of a substance are dispersed in another substance, they are not mixed or dissolved but are held in suspension. When the particles are very small, the suspension is called a colloid.

When the colloid is a liquid suspended in another liquid, an example could be mayonnaise, an emulsion is formed.

Shaving foam is a colloid of air dispersed in a liquid.

Fog is a colloid of water vapour dispersed in the air.

Super Challenge

How would you separate pure water from a mixture of sea water (salt and water), and sand?

Reversible and Irreversible Changes

Reversible means it can go back to what it was before.

When chocolate is heated, it melts.

When this cools down it returns as a solid.

solid chocolate $\xrightarrow[\text{cools}]{\text{heat}}$ liquid chocolate.

This is a reversible reaction.

The original objects have returned to what it was before being heated.

When bread is heated, it loses some water, becomes brown and is called toast.

If it is heated too long, at too high a temperature, it may burn. When this cools down, it remains as toast.

Bread + heat $\longrightarrow$ toast.

This is a permanent change, and is an irreversible change.

Think with Spike

Which type of reaction: reversible, or irreversible is represented by heating, dissolving or mixing the following:

Chocolate melting

Metal rusting

Ice melting

Salt dissolving

Paper burning

An egg frying

Dried fruit mixed

In chemistry, a reversible and irreversible reaction can often occur at the same time.

The reaction would continue until all the initial reactants are used up, which could not happen if it occurred in a stoppered reaction tube, (care would be needed with this due to a build-up of pressure), do not try this!

An example being unstable ammonium chloride.

ammonium chloride (s) $\xrightarrow[\text{products cooled and recorded one}]{\text{gently heated}}$ ammonia (g) + hydrogen chloride (g)

(s) solid (g) gas.

$NH_4Cl (s) \xrightarrow[\text{products cooled and recorded one}]{\text{gently heated}} NH_3 (g) + HCl (g)$

An irreversible reaction would be the effects of temperature and pressure on limestone rock.

Limestone $\xrightarrow[\text{pressure}]{\text{temperature}}$ marble.

The result of this creating a new material.

Physical Properties

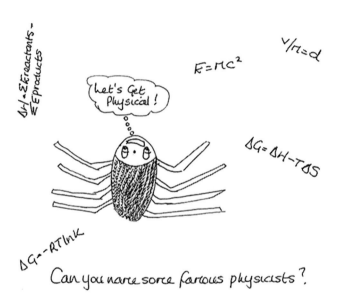

Force and Magnets

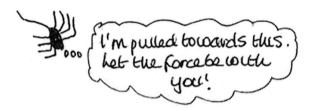

Forces can be balanced or unbalanced.

They involve a push pull action and change the state of rest of the total motion of an object, or change the direction or shape of an object.

To achieve this, two objects need to interact.

The two forces act in opposite directions on an object and are equal in size and extend: magnitude.

An unbalanced force, for example, more of a push than a pull force, would increase the momentum of the objects, causing it to move in the direction of the pushing force.

Balanced forces keep the object stationary.

Force is always indicated by an arrow, which indicates magnitudes and direction.

Push —▶ ◀— pull (unbalanced force).

There is more of a pushing force than a pulling force.

Push —▶ ◀— Pull (balanced force)

The pushing and pulling forces are equal.

A normal force has equal magnitude and works in an opposite direction to gravity on an object.

Friction will prevent and restrict motion; more on this later.

Push ——▶ ◀—— pull being balanced and equal, there is no acceleration, they cancel each other out and the resulting force, measured in Newtons, after a very famous, Sir Isaac Newton, (4 Jan 1643-Mar 1727), is on, (zero newtons).

Forces include: normal, applied, friction, tension, spring and resistance.

Newton gave us the law of inertia. This is a resistance of change from the original motion or rest.

The greater the mass, the greater the inertia, the greater the resistance to change.

93

The family cat, princess perfect, was up in the apple tree the other day. How did she manage to stay there and sleep among the branches?

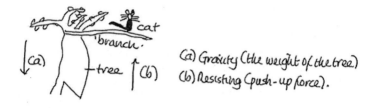

(a) Gravity (the weight of the tree)
(b) Resisting (push-up force).

As the cat sleeps, there is no change in force.
As soon as the cat moves, there is a change in force.

Think with Spike

We will work on these together. They have some extra questions for us to think about.

A light hanging from the ceiling:

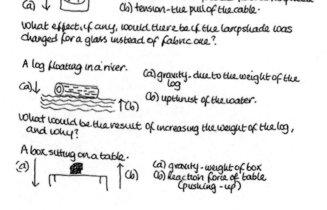

(a) gravity - due to the weight of the glass bulb and metal-framed fabric lampshade
(b) tension - the pull of the cable.

What effect, if any, would there be if the lampshade was changed for a glass instead of fabric one?

A log floating in a river.

(a) gravity - due to the weight of the log
(b) upthrust of the water.

What would be the result of increasing the weight of the log, and why?

A box sitting on a table.

(a) gravity - weight of box
(b) reaction force of table (pushing-up)

What would happen if the box was moved to the edge of the table, with some overhanging the edge?

What effect does this have on force?

We already covered some work on magnets earlier.

Due to the magnetic field, a magnet does not need to touch an object for a force to occur.

As my previous diagram showed:

A north pole will attract a south pole.

A south pole will attract a north pole.

A north pole will repel a north pole.

A south pole will repel a south pole.

An experiment to investigate what a magnet will be attracted to, will it repel or will it do nothing?

With a magnet, see the effects of placing it near metal/ steel paperclip, a piece of stone, some aluminium foil, a wooden chair, a tin can, a jam jar lid, a plastic spoon, an iron key, another magnet checking both poles.

Can you present your results in a table?

What do you notice?

Super Challenge

Could you devise a game using magnets? What would the purpose of it be?

Which age group would it be aimed at?

Friction

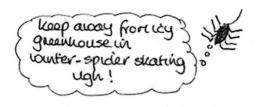

Keep away from icy
greenhouse in
winter- spider skating
ugh!

Friction is a force. It is measured in Newtons.

It is the resistance of motion, when one object rubs against another. Anytime two objects rub against each other, they cause friction.

Friction works against the motion or applied force and acts in the opposite direction.

When wooden sticks or flints are rubbed together to start a fire, the kinetic energy is converted to thermal energy (heat). The molecules on the surfaces being rubbed move faster and create more energy.

When one object is sliding on another, it starts to slow down due to friction.

Thinking of atoms, we can say that friction is the result of electromagnetic attraction between two charged particles on two touching surfaces.

The positively charged being attracted to the negatively charged.

Friction depends on SMOOTHNESS and the WEIGHT of the object or the amount of force on the surface.

Spike Says:

A greater force is needed to move two surfaces past one another if they are rough rather than smooth.

Friction does not depend on X, the area of the surfaces, or the sliding speed, X.

Friction is directly proportional to the weight of the load moving.

DOUBLE the weight would mean DOUBLE the friction factor.

Heavier objects have move friction force because they are pressed more tightly together.

Air and Water Resistance

The wind nearly blew me and my web away; that took some resisting!

A friction force where moving objects rub against molecules of the gases that make up the air or the water molecules is called resistance

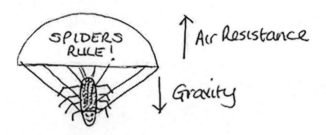

As my parachute indicates, the air resistance which acts against gravity increases as my parachute is opened, and in turn, this slows me down.

Air resistance always acts in the opposite direction to the object's motion.

Air resistance depends on VELOCITY and CROSS-SECTIONAL AREA.

Spike Says:

The faster the motion, the greater the air resistance against it.

Air particles hit the front of an object, slowing it down.

A similar effect is felt in water.

The higher the surface area of an object, the move particles will hit it and the greater the resistance, the slower the speed.

It also depends on the SHAPE of the object and the DENSITY of the air, (altitude, temperature and humidity).

A heavy object increases air resistance to equal its weight.

To increase air resistance, more speed is required and this is why heavy objects fall faster in air than lighter ones.

Air resistance acts constantly through motion and is never cancelled.

In a heavy wind, the air has high resistance as it pushes against you.

Think with Spike

Holding an open umbrella on a windy day:

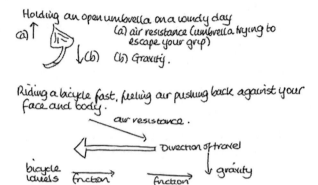

Holding an open umbrella on a windy day
(a) air resistance (umbrella trying to escape your grip)
(b) Gravity.

Riding a bicycle fast, feeling air pushing back against your face and body.

air resistance.

Direction of travel

bicycle wheels   friction   friction   gravity

When the rider crouches down low and wears a streamlined helmet, they reduce air resistance.

If the peed is increase X two the opposing air resistance increases X four.

(X=times)

A bicycle speeding up has an equal force pushing the bicycle forward: when the two forces become balanced, it will reach a steady speed; its terminal velocity.

A feather, or leaf, floating to the ground:

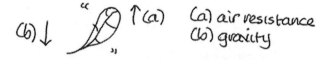

(a) air resistance
(b) gravity

The leaf floats as the gravitational force is low and air is everywhere, increasing air resistance.

As it is light, the leaf fails slower and the air gets in the object's way.

Reducing Air Resistance

An aeroplane involves several forces.

These include: thrust, air resistance, lift and gravity.

The engine and propellers produce thrust to overcome air resistance.

Thrust pushes the aeroplane through the air

The wing produces lift to overcome gravity.

Forces and a paper plane:

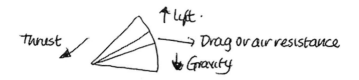

Think with Spike

If you take a sheet of paper and a screwed-up ball of paper and drop them from the same height at the same time what would happen?

Which would land first? Why?

Superstar Challenge

Could you create an experiment to prove s streamlining in water? Apparatus could include water, a large beaker, a stop watch and shapes made out of modelling clay, for example, cubes, triangles, stars, tear-shaped, etc.

To ensure it is a fair test, each shape must weigh the same. So, you will also need some scales.

Gravity

All the planets in the solar system remain in orbit due to gravitational force.

The gravitational force between an object and a planet, which pulls the objects downwards, is the weight of the object.

Scientist, Sir Isaac Newton (1643–1727), gave us a law of gravitation. There is a gravitational pull between two objects depend on the object's mass and distance between them.

Spike Says:

Did you know a balance (or scales), actually measures the force pushed upon them? The scale translates this to mass.

At the surface of the earth, 100 kg=980 N (Newtons)

On the surface of the moon, 100 kg=160 N

10,000 km above the earth, 100 kg=150 N

This is because weight is not constant, but depends on the distance from, and the mass of the planet.

Around the earth, gravity is a force pulling the planet inwards and creating the sphere shape.

The atoms all pull towards a common centre of gravity and are resisted outwards by a force holding them apart.

This can be represented by:

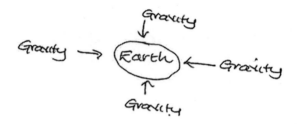

This is the reason why an apple falling from a tree will fall to the ground. The force of gravity is pulling the apple towards the earth.

Even when it is on the ground, gravity still pulls the apple down towards the earth. If it did not, then it may float away.

Levers, Pulleys and Gears

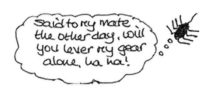

A lever is any rigid object which moves, or pivots about a point, or axis, called the FULCRUM (f).

The load, the object being lifted and moved, and the effort, the work being used to actually move it, can be on opposite, or the same sides.

For example, a teaspoon of coffee balancing on a coffee jar:

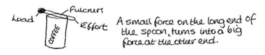

Load   Fulcrum   Effort   A small force on the long end of the spoon, turns into a big force at the other end.

Similarly, with a pulley system.
The load force is applied at one point and the effort at another point.

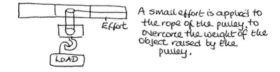

Effort   A small effort is applied to the rope of the pulley, to overcome the weight of the object raised by the pulley.

105

Spike Says:

Did you know, the force needed to overcome friction within moving parts of a machine, like the one above, and to raise its moving parts is called useless load?

Gears are a vital part of many machines.

They are found in bicycles and clocks, (their mechanism), cars, vacuum cleaners, etc.

Gears transmit power from one part of a machine to another.

A cog is one of the teeth on awheel or gear that, via other teeth, transmit or receive motion.

Spike Says:

Did you know that a gear is a wheel with cogs that work with gears of another wheel?

A sprocket is a wheel with cogs that work with a chain, for example:

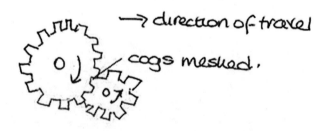

This is why it is hard to push a heavy box around a carpeted room.

With a SOLID, the strongest friction force is

STATIC: nothing is moving

Then is, SLIDING, the surfaces are touching, but some movement is allowed.

The weakest is, ROLLING, the surfaces meet but movement continues.

With a FLUID or GAS, the friction force is DRAG or AIR/WATER RESISTANCE.

Think with Spike

What makes a car slow down at a stop sign and causes friction?

If you wear shoes and walk on a carpet, why do you not slip?

Predict what will happen.

Rub your hands together.

First gently and slowly. Then get harder and quicker.

Does this match your prediction?

Rub together again with wet and soapy hands, what happens?

Is there a difference? Why?

Superstar Challenge

How does an ice-skater keep skating?

What is meant by the term lubrication and how does this apply to this?

Electricity

Electricity is the movement of electrons around a circuit.

Circuit and Conductors

In your house, there is a mains electric supply. This is produced at power-stations by huge generators.

Alternating current is generated and transformers transform this to high voltage and low current electrical power, which reduces power loss in the cables and is safer.

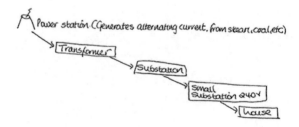

The main electric supply is 240 V (volts).

Appliances using mains electricity include toasters, fridges and washing machines.

Those which use batteries can include clocks, calculators and smoke alarms.

In electricity the current is represented by I, and is the rate of flow of the electric charge.

In a circuit, there is a difference in potential in two places, between these places, this potential difference produces a current, and is represented as Volts.

A circuit is a closed loop, consisting of a source of potential difference and component (s), around which current flows.

In a circuit, the wire and crocodile clips are used to link the parts of the circuit together and have to be made of a conducting material, e.g. copper.

The cell, with a positive and negative terminal, provides the power source for the circuit.

A switch turns the flow of electricity on and off.

When it is off, electrons are unable to flow, as the circuit is no longer a closed loop.

A bulb would give out light and heat. It would only work when the circuit is complete.

Think like Spike

Could you create a circuit to identify conductors and insulators?

Remember to use light bulbs to help indicate that the circuit is working correctly, and has been set up correctly.

Items tested would include a wooden block, a plastic spoon, a steel spoon, some fabric, and some coinage

How would you know that the material was a conductor?

What would you see?

Could you represent your results in a table?

How could you make this a fair representation of conductors and insulators?

What do you conclude?

Circuit Diagrams

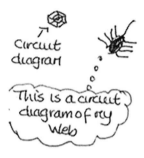

Circuit diagram

This is a circuit diagram of my Web

Electric circuits are represented in circuit diagrams,

Different components involved can be shown as:

cell   buzzer   bulb   switch (off)   motor

A simple circuit diagram representing three cells, 2 switches (off) and 2 bulbs:

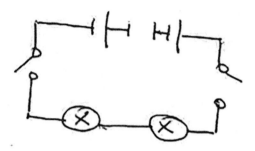

A simple circuit diagram representing two cells, a motor and a switch (on):

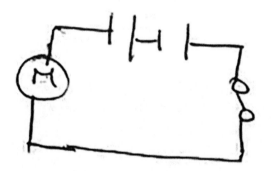

To make a bulb in a circuit dimmer, either remove one of the cells, or add another bulb; this reduces the number of electrons and current reaching one bulb.

The higher the voltage of a cell, the brighter, louder or faster the components; bulb, buzzer or motor, would become.

The more components that are added to a circuit, the less power each shall receive from the cell.

How We See Things

My eight eyes help me see everything.

Remember: never look directly at the sun!

Light waves travel in straight lines to an object.

The object gives out/ refracts/ light into the eyes, which is then reflected.

Refraction is the change in direction of a wave as its velocity changes when it moves from one medium to another, for example from air to water.

When moved into a dense medium (water), the waves are slowed down and become refracted.

The straw appears bent in this diagram because the light waves have been refracted by the liquid as it changed medium from air to liquid.

Reflection is dealt with in the next chapter.

Light travels from light sources to our eyes or from light sources to objects to our eyes.

A transparent material would allow all light waves through.

An opaque material blocks the waves and absorbs them.

Light source:

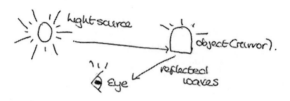

A Simple Diagram of the Eye:

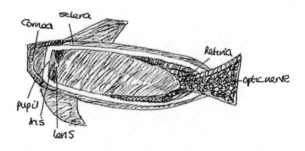

Light waves enter through the pupil, the size being changed by the iris. This lets more/less light in and hence protects or maximises the amount of light.

Light waves travel through to the retina, which contains special cells called rods and cones.

The cones help to detect colour.

From the retina, an electrical impulse passes along the optic nerve to the brain. The image is then inverted, after being sent to the brain upside-down.

Superstar Challenge

Why do we see objects of a particular colour, for example, green grass?

What is white light actually composed of?

Mirror and Reflections

Reflection is the change in direction of a light/sound wave when it bounces off an object.

Mirrors show the reflection of light.

When an object and its image are drawn in a mirror diagram, the light waves still come from a light source, for example, the sun, and are reflected off the object.

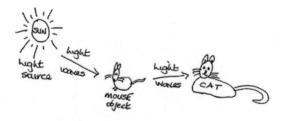

A Periscope

This uses mirrors and reflection to help see objects which are further away.

It works in the following way:

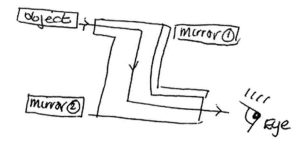

Light waves from the object are reflected off the mirror.

(1) They pass down the periscope to mirror.
(2) Where they are reflected off the mirror and pass through the last part of the periscope to the eye.

Think like Spike

Could you build a periscope?
Could you prove how it waves?

Shadows

Earth's natural light source is the sun.

Earth orbits round the sun, and as the earth turns on its axis, we have day and night.

Shadows are seen by other light sources too.

Candles, torches and electric lights, being examples.

A shadow is formed when light travelling in straight lines, from a light source is blocked by an opaque object.

The object itself absorbs all the light waves.

Distance between the object and the light source affects the size of the shadow.

The further away the light sources are from the object, the smaller the shadow gets.

Sound

Sound travels in waves, caused by vibrations in the air.

A scientific instrument called an oscilloscope, draws an electronic graph on a screen; converting sound energy from a microphone into an electrical signal. This signal is shown as the graph or picture on the screen.

Amplitude is how loud sound is.

Frequency is the speed or occurrence of the vibration and this, in turn, determines pitch.

A whistle, or a tuning fork, would produce a smooth and regular pattern.

Many frequencies mixed together would produce jagged lines.

Spike Says:

High notes at high frequency, the waves are close together.

Low notes at low frequency, the waves are spread out.

Think like Spike

Try making your own string telephones.
Two plastic cups with small holes in the bottom.

Thread string through and tie the end in the bottoms of each cup.

With a friend, whisper into the cup and hear what they say.

How do string telephones work?

When you talk, your voice vibrates in your voice box.

The sound waves vibrate through the air into the cup held in front of the speaker's mouth

The vibrations in the air inside the cup then vibrate the string and vibrate the air inside the cup next to the listener's ear.

These vibrations travel through the air and are converted into sound.

In order for sound to be heard, the string needs to be kept taut.

This means very straight and tight.

This also means you can hear around corners.

Superstar Challenge

Does sound travel in a vacuum? And can you hear it? Why?

Sound Distance

As distance from the sound source increases, the area covered by the sound waves increases.

The same amount of sound energy is spread over a greater area, with the intensity and loudness getting less. This is why loud sounds fade away as they get farther from the source.

Sound levels decrease with distance, due to absorption.

Sound travels through the medium, for example, air or water, and becomes caught by the molecules in the medium and absorbed.

Some sound energy is also changed to heat.

In water

Sound waves spread out. Some energy absorbed by water.

Eventually, sound is gone, as the medium's molecules vibrate less and less in the jostle of the medium's molecules.

Think like Spike

How can you hear a fire-engine coming and know which direction it is coming from?

Spike Says:

Did you know that the pitch of a sound is dictated by the frequency of the sound wave?

The loudness by the amplitude.

A high pitch sound corresponds to a high frequency sound wave and a low pitch sound to a low frequency sound wave.

In a guitar, the length, diameter, tension and density of a string affect pitch.

When the length of a string is changed; it will vibrate with a different frequency.

Shorter strings have higher frequencies and higher pitch.

Earth, Sun and Moon

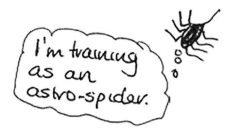

The earth, sun and the moon are part of a solar system.

The sun is at the centre of the solar system, but appears to change its position during the day.

Earth orbits around the sun and is the third planet out from the centre of the solar system.

In term, the rocky moon is earth's natural satellite, and it orbits around the earth, and also the sun.

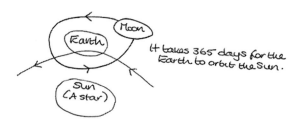

It takes 28 days for the moon to orbit the earth.

Earth itself is a sphere, which spins round and round, as it travels around the sun.

One side of the earth faces the sun, while the other faces away into space. The side facing the sun is bathed in light and heat: day time.

The side facing away is cooler and darker: night

The planets in the solar system are in an order as they orbit around the sun, the closest to the sun is Mercury, then Venus, Earth, Mars Jupiter, Saturn, Uranus and Neptune.

Superstar Challenge

What effect does the relationship between earth, sun and moon have on the sides? Tides?

Spike Says:

Did you know that over a million earths would fill inside the centre of the sun?

Spider Facts

Spiders are found in every continent except Antarctica.

There are around 40,000 different species of spider.

An estimated 1 million spiders live in one acre of land.

A human is never more than ten feet away from a spider.

Spiders eat more insects than bats and birds combined.

When a spider travels, it always has four legs touching the ground and four legs off the ground at any given moment.

Unlike humans with iron as the mineral in their blood, spiders have copper.

A spider's muscles pull it legs inward, but cannot extend them out again. Instead, it pumps a watery liquid into its legs to push them out.

Scientists cannot replicate the strength and elasticity of spider's silk.

Some male spiders give dead flies to females as presents.

Tiny hairs on their legs help them hear and smell.

A strand of spider silk, long enough to go around the earth, would weigh just over 1 lb.

Super Scientific Words

(In order found in the book and explained in detail in the text)
LIVING THINGS
Flora: A plant
Leaves
Roots
Stem
Flower
Bulb
What Fiona Needs to Be Healthy
Light energy
Photosynthesis
Formula
Nutrients
Minerals
Water
Turgid
Wilting
Air
Stomata
Diffused
Compete
Fair test

Prediction

Translocation

Transpiration

Flowers and Reproduction

Sepal

Petals

Stamen

Carpel

Nectar

Pollination

Fertilization

Seed Dispersal

Competition

Overcrowding

Classification

Cephalothorax

Features

Lungs

Organisms

Habitat

Vertebrates

Exoskeleton

Endoskeleton

Invertebrates

Arachnid

Environment

Biodiversity

Ecosystem

Habitat

Eco-friendly

Nuche

Pollute

Acid rain

Natural alternatives

Recycles

Nature Reserves

Life cycle-Plants

Stigma

Fertilization

Sexual reproduction

Asexually

Runners

Offsets

Micro environment

Life cycle-Animals

Sperm

Ova

Gestation

Pregnant

Birth

Life cycle-Humans

Baby

Toddler

Child

Puberty

Adolescent

Adult

Old age

Hormones

Bones and Muscles

Exoskeleton

Endoskeleton

Support

Protect

Spinal cord

Joint

Cartilage

Contracts

Relaxes

Antagonistic

Circulation and Heart Systemic

Pulmonary (system-circulation)

Lumen

Valves

Diffusion

Iron

Nuclei

Biconcave

Oxygenated

Bronchioles

Bronchus

Alveoli

Gravity

Precordium Pericardium

Cardiac

Mistral

Bicuspid

Aortic

Pulmonary (valves)

Blood pressure

Teeth and eating

Permanent teeth

Tooth decay

Plaque

Premolar

Wisdom teeth

Carnivore

Omnivore

Herbivore

Digestion

Oesophagus

Stomach

Pyloric sphincter

Small intestine

Lacteal

Large intestine

Peristalsis

Enzymes

Specific

Optimum

Healthy living

Balanced diet

Nutrients

Trace minerals

Trace elements

Anaemia

Hydrated

Soluble

Insoluble

Food Chains

Bio diverse ecosystem

Food web

Dependant

Interdependent

Producer

Consumer

Primary consumer

Secondary consumer

Tertiary consumer

Quaternary consumer

Prey

Predator

Venation Variation

Offspring

Inherited

Variation

Cells

Genes

Dominant

Adaption

Habitats

Evolve

Extinct

Genes

Camouflage

Specialised

General

Physical

Behavioural

Nocturnal

Hibernate

Social

Solitary

Fossils and evolution

Sedimentary

Preserved

Strata

Trace fossils

Amber

Palaeontologist

Materials and their Properties

Rocks

Rock cycle

Tectonic plates

Lava

Magma

Igneous

Sedimentary

Metamorphic

Hard

Impermeable

Soft

Permeable

Soil

Weathering

Fragments

Clay

Silt

Sand

Invertebrates

Microbes

Erodes

Physical change

Chemical change

Biological change

Horizons

Components

Solid, liquid and gas

States of water

Atoms

Viscous

Density

Air

Water vapour

Changing states

Irreversible change

Reversible change

Melting point

Annotated

Melts

Evaporates

Water droplets

Condense

Freezes

Sublimation

Ionises

Thermal

Water cycle

Evaporated

Humid

Surface area

Properties of materials

Conductors

Insulators

(Electric conductivity and materials)

Electrons

Electric charge

Static electricity

Electromagnetism

Separating mixtures

Sieve

Dissolving

Saturated solution

Solute

Solvent

Solution

Dissolved

Evaporates

Condenses

Purr Pure

Insoluble

Filter

Precipitate

Filtrate

Miscible

Diffusion

Immiscible

Dispersed

Suspension

Colloid

Emulsion

Reversible and irreversible changes

Heated

Reversible

Permanent

Irreversible changes

Reactants

PHYSICAL PROPERTIES

Force and magnets

Balanced

Unbalanced

State of rest

Direction

Shape

Magnitude

Stationary

Gravity

Friction

Kinetic energy

Thermal energy

Weight

Air and water resistance

Streamlined

Terminal velocity

Gravity

Orbit

Weight

Levers, pulleys, and gears

Pivot

Axis

Fulcrum

Load

Effort

Useless load

Cog

Sprocket

Electricity-circuits and Conductors

Mains electric supply

Generators

Transformers

Alternating currents

Batteries

Currents

Potential difference

Volts

Circuit

Conducting

How we see things

Refraction

Reflection

Diffuse

Pupil

Iris

Inverted

Shadows

Orbits

Axis

Sound

Waves

Vibrations

Oscilloscope

Amplitude

Frequency

Pitch

Taut

Absorption

Earth, Sun and Moon

Solar system

Orbits satellite

Bibliography

The Usborne Illustrated Dictionary of Science
    A Complete Reference Guide to Physics, Chemistry and
Biology

Superstar Challenge

All challenges attempted, can be emailed to the author at ann.dale1966@gmail.com, or forwarded to the publisher.

Real superstars will be awarded super spidery scientific prizes.